A Shelter in Our Car

**Story
Monica Gunning**

**Illustrations
Elaine Pedlar**

A Shelter in Our Car

Story
Monica Gunning

Illustrations
Elaine Pedlar

Children's Book Press • *an imprint of* Lee & Low Books Inc.
New York

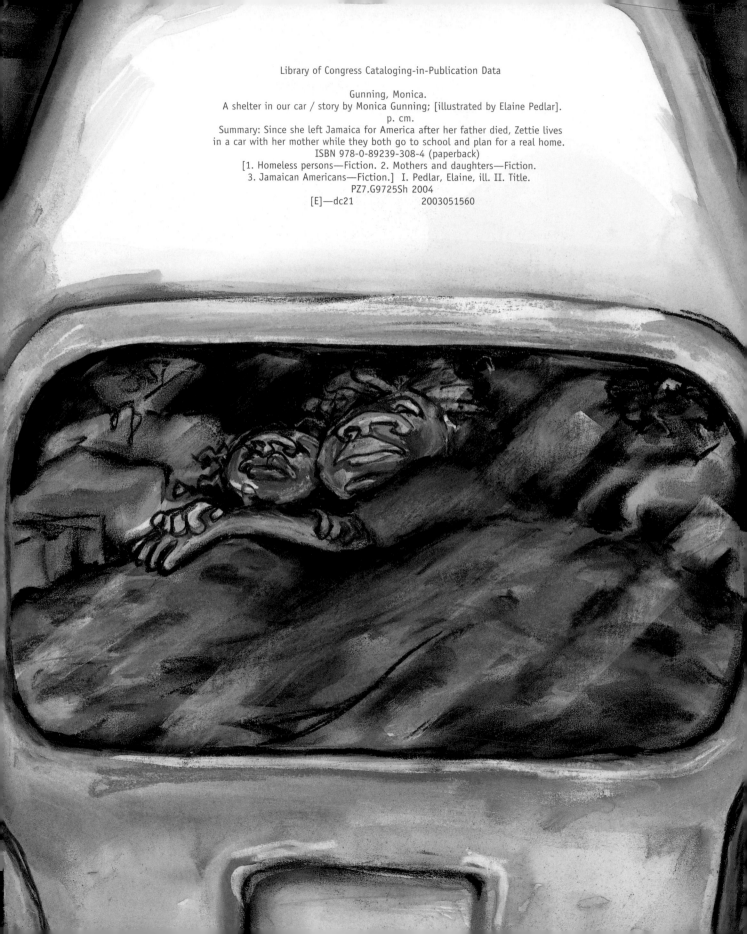

Library of Congress Cataloging-in-Publication Data

Gunning, Monica.
A shelter in our car / story by Monica Gunning; [illustrated by Elaine Pedlar].
p. cm.
Summary: Since she left Jamaica for America after her father died, Zettie lives
in a car with her mother while they both go to school and plan for a real home.
ISBN 978-0-89239-308-4 (paperback)
[1. Homeless persons—Fiction. 2. Mothers and daughters—Fiction.
3. Jamaican Americans—Fiction.] I. Pedlar, Elaine, ill. II. Title.
PZ7.G9725Sh 2004
[E]—dc21   2003051560

This book is dedicated to
my first granddaughter, Elon Gunning.
—Monica Gunning

I dedicate this book to my family and
to all families that, like Zettie and her mom,
realize that the greatest shelter of all is love.
—Elaine Pedlar

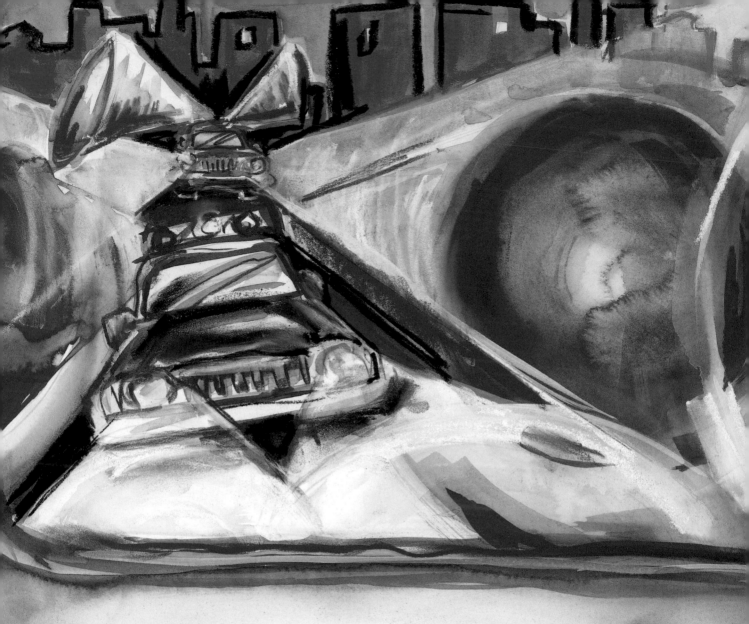

Police cars are coming closer! The sirens hurt my ears and the lights blind my eyes. I jump up, really, really frightened.

"Shhh, Zettie, lie down," Mama says. "We don't want to be noticed."

We sink between the clothes on the back seat of the car. "Mama, it's creepy sleeping in our car," I whisper.

"I know," she says. "Things happen in the city. Police cars are always on some kind of chase."

She holds me close until the sirens stop.

When all is quiet, Mama drives down Chandler Avenue and parks in front of a courtyard apartment house. Its garden is filled with flowers—bougainvilleas, roses, hibiscus--in the streetlight, their colors as bright as the flowers in the yard we left behind in Port Antonio. Mama and I love parking in this spot.

For weeks, a For Rent sign has hung in one of the windows. We asked about it last week, but the owner told us he'd only rent to someone with a steady job. And he wants the first and last months' rent, which Mama doesn't have.

I close my eyes. Soon I'm in dreamland, back home in Jamaica with Papa and Grandma Mullins. We're picnicking on the beach. Waves pound against the rocks. Crash, bang! I wake up. No, I'm not in Jamaica. I'm in America. And it's not the waves crashing against rocks. Someone's knocking on our car window.

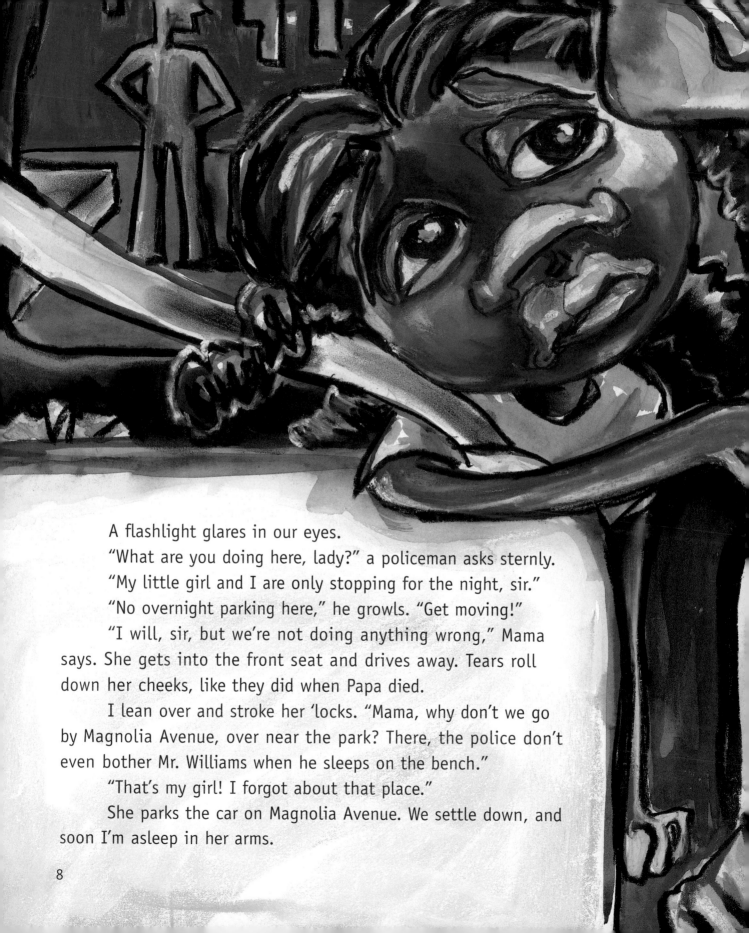

A flashlight glares in our eyes.

"What are you doing here, lady?" a policeman asks sternly.

"My little girl and I are only stopping for the night, sir."

"No overnight parking here," he growls. "Get moving!"

"I will, sir, but we're not doing anything wrong," Mama says. She gets into the front seat and drives away. Tears roll down her cheeks, like they did when Papa died.

I lean over and stroke her 'locks. "Mama, why don't we go by Magnolia Avenue, over near the park? There, the police don't even bother Mr. Williams when he sleeps on the bench."

"That's my girl! I forgot about that place."

She parks the car on Magnolia Avenue. We settle down, and soon I'm asleep in her arms.

Early next morning, Mama wakes me up and reminds me, "Let's use the rest room in the park before it gets crowded."

It's chilly there, and I shiver as I put on my school clothes. Then I splash water on my face from the faucet.

"Mama, this water is cold as ice."

"Try to be brave," she whispers.

We go outside and sit down on a bench. Mama braids my hair in four plats, the way I like it, but she pulls hard to make it look just right. I start singing a song I made up, trying not to notice when she yanks too hard.

For a while Mama hums along, but when I sing louder, she puts a finger to her lips.

"Not so loud, Zettie. You'll wake Mr. Williams."

Mama opens our little ice chest and makes peanut butter and jelly sandwiches. We drink some leftover orange soda. It's sweet, but flat. We've had it for three days.

"I wish we had some hot chocolate," I say. "The kind you used to make from the cocoa beans we picked near home."

"It makes me sad that you don't have some." She looks into my eyes. "Do you remember the sun in Jamaica?" Mama asks. "How brightly it shone after a shower of rain?"

I do remember. Especially on cold, cloudy days like today. Why did Papa have to die? With Mama's now-and-then day jobs and her working so hard going to community college, it's like having dark, wet days all the time.

"When I get a steady job there'll be sunshine again," Mama says, as if she read my mind.

I'm silent. I hear that from Mama all the time, but things are so hard now.

On the way to school, I say, "Mama, could you . . . "

"What is it, Zettie?"

"Could you drop me off at the corner behind the school?"

"Why?" she asks.

"Mean boys say our car is old and junky. They make fun of the flag in the window. Why do you have to keep it there, Mama?" I snap.

She pulls over and hugs me. "Pay them no mind, my child. Get your book learning just like your Papa did, and hold your head high. I'll take down the flag."

I hurry out of the car to get away. "I'll wait for you on the playground after school," I call out over my shoulder.

Mama picks me up after school. I duck my head into my jacket so no one will recognize me as I scurry into the car.

"There were no office jobs at the Temporary Agency today," Mama tells me.

"Does that mean we'll eat peanut butter and jelly again tonight?" I grumble and turn my whole body away from her.

"No! I did something else, though. Guess what?"

"I don't care," I say. "We'll never get an apartment if you don't get a steady job!"

"I handed out fliers at a Health Fair. Didn't make much money, but I have enough to buy some supper and some gas for the car."

My face feels hot and my chest is tight. Why can't Mama do some other kind of work?

My tummy growls. I begin to forget about being angry. "Can we get hot dogs and buns to share with Ana Mae and Benjie at the park?"

When we arrive, Benjie runs up to me. He's eight, just like I am, but small and bony. Mama makes us all some dinner. His eyes shine when he sees the hot dogs, and I wonder if he has eaten anything today.

"Want to come with me to look for empty cans and bottles to sell?" Benjie asks afterwards.

"I don't know . . . " I say. Mama watches me pretty closely and doesn't like my rummaging around. Benjie is saving money from the cans and bottles we sell, to help his mother. He already has $1.50.

"Stay where I can see you, and be careful," Mama calls. Benjie runs around and between the trees looking for thrown-away bottles and cans. He starts to dig into the garbage cans to find some. But I tell him that's dangerous, that he can't tell what might be inside, and he stops.

We're happy with Benjie's pile today. He'll probably make another dollar.

"You're my best friend," Benjie tells me as he waves good-bye.

"You are mine too," I say.

That night Mama and I curl up on the back seat of the car and Mama reads to me from a book we got at the library.

"Sleeping in the car is better than at the church shelter," I tell Mama. "I hated that noisy, crowded place! A baby cried the whole time. Remember?"

"That's why I'd rather use our car as a shelter, Zettie," she answers.

I snuggle beside her and she begins to study for one of her exams.

The next day after school, I read my book as I wait for Mama on the playground. Just as I turn the page, Alex the bully sneaks up behind me and yanks my plats.

"Junk Car Zettie!" he teases. "Watch out for Junk Car Zettie!" he calls to his friends. They all laugh and yell it out real loud, "Junk Car Zettie!"

"Dumbbells!" I snap at the boys.

That makes them really angry. Alex pulls my plats again, hard!

I'm scared now.
Not a teacher around
anywhere. What should
I do? Finally, I run, faster
than I ever thought I could
run. Away from the playground,
down the street to a far corner.
Now they can't see me.

23

I'm out of breath and panting when I see Mama drive up the street next to the school gate. She gets out of the car to look for me.

"Mama! Mama!" I call, waving to get her attention, but she doesn't see me. She gets back into the car and turns around. I shout louder and run toward her, but I trip and she drives away.

My knee is skinned and bleeding. I put some spit on it and hobble back to the corner. Then I sit down and cry. Our lives have changed so much since Papa died . . .

I wait for a while, my eyes still on the playground, but Mama doesn't return. Where did Mama go? Knowing that she's out looking for me only makes me cry harder.

I open my eyes to the whirr of a motorcycle stopping. It's a policeman! Am I in trouble?

He asks, "Are you lost?"

"No, sir. My mama is late picking me up."

"I can't leave you here alone," he says. He sounds kind.

He stays close to watch me . . . but not too close. I didn't know a policeman could be so nice. I thought they were all mean like that one who shouted at Mama and made her cry that night.

It seems like forever that I wait. I only have Mama now, I think. Where is she? What will happen to me if anything happens to her? Will the policeman have to place me in a foster home? Living in a car isn't the best thing in the world, but at least I've had Mama loving me and taking care of me.

Then I hear a car honking.

It's Mama. Tears spatter her face. She cries, "Why did you leave the playground, Zettie? Why?"

Sobbing, I tell her what happened.

"I was scared, Mama. That's why I ran down here."

"I thought you went to the park," she continues. "Benjie and Ana Mae helped me look for you. We were all so worried. Thank goodness you're safe." She waves to the policeman to let him know everything's okay.

Between tears, I force a smile, happy that Mama's with me again. Her eyes are still red. I can tell she was crying a lot, worrying about me.

She puts her arm around me. "We both need to relax tonight," she says. "I worked a long day at the Health Fair again and they paid me for more hours. Let's celebrate this evening."

We drive to a cafeteria for spaghetti and ice cream.

After supper, Mama winks. "Surprise! We'll sleep in a real bed tonight."

"In a motel? That really comfy one we slept in last time?" I cry out.

As soon as we check into our room, I dash
inside the bathroom and turn on the shower. The water tickles
my back.

"Oh Mama, warm water feels sooo good! I wish I could have
a shower every day."

When I jump into bed, I stretch out, wiggle my toes and
bring the clean sheet up to my nose. Mama hugs me and calls me
Buttercup, and I can feel her love washing over me.

"How would you like to sleep in a bed all summer instead of
in our car?" she asks.

"At the Health Fair, the woman there offered me a job. I'm going to help in a program for people like us, people who work hard to find homes. We'll be able to afford a room," Mama explains.

"Oh, Mama! Will you be able to save for that courtyard apartment while you work there? And study too?"

"I hope so," she says and hugs me tighter.

I nestle in her arms. "Mama, I'm sorry for being mean sometimes." Then I snuggle closer and fall asleep, knowing that, with or without an apartment, I've got Mama and she's got me.

Homelessness in America

What basic things do all human beings need to survive? We need love, food, clothing, education, and—very, very importantly—we need a safe place to live, a place to shelter us from rain, snow, sun, and wind, a place where we can grow and blossom. But many children in this country do not have such a place.

According to the National Alliance to End Homelessness, about 3 million people in the United States don't have homes at some time during the year. Close to half of these people are families with children. Some of them live on the street, some in shelters, in campgrounds, or with other family members or friends. And some, like the mother and daughter in this story, live in their cars.

Some people are homeless because they are ill or can't find work, and so can't afford a place to live. Many people who work hard every day find housing costs are more than they can afford. But whatever the reason, homelessness can be remedied. How can you help? Research the problem in your community and share what you learn with other people; find out about organizations that work with persons without homes and ask what you can do to help; work with your school to organize a clothing drive . . . Each one of us can be part of the solution to this very serious problem.

Photo by Bill Johnson

Monica Gunning

was born in Jamaica, West Indies, and immigrated to the United States to work and further her education. After graduating from the City University in New York and from Mount Saint Mary's College in Los Angeles, she became a teacher in the Los Angeles Unified School District. The author of two critically acclaimed books of poetry for children, *Not a Copper Penny in Me House* and *Under the Breadfruit Tree,* she has also published extensively in magazines and anthologies. Ms. Gunning is the proud mother of two sons, Michael and Mark, and has four grandchildren.

Photo by Brian Sullivan

Elaine Pedlar

was born in Rockaway Beach, Queens, New York, the youngest girl of seven children. She graduated from Parsons School of Design in 1987 and, since then, has been a fashion designer. Illustrating books for children has been her constant dream, however, and *A Shelter in Our Car* was her first opportunity to make it come true. Single and living in a loft in Brooklyn, she has nine nieces and nephews that she loves dearly.

Children's Book Press, an imprint of LEE & LOW BOOKS Inc., 95 Madison Avenue, New York, NY 10016, leeandlow.com

FSC
www.fsc.org
MIX
Paper from responsible sources
FSC® C012700

Book design: Aileen Friedman
Book production: The Kids at Our House
Book editors: Ina Cumpiano, Dana Goldberg

Our thanks to April Silas of the Homeless Children's Network of San Francisco.

Manufactured in Malaysia by Tien Wah Press
10 9 8 7 6
First Edition

$10.95 US

Praise for **A Shelter in Our Car**

"Not since Maurice Sendak's *We Are All in the Dumps with Jack and Guy* has a picture book dealing with homelessness maintained such emotional intensity...Children will be moved by Zettie's plight and relieved that there are options."   —School Library Journal

"Readers will find eye-opening both Gunning's well-chosen details and Pedlar's brooding, expressionistic art."   —Horn Book Guide

"This is a book to open the eyes and hearts of readers 6 and older."
—Tampa Tribune

ISBN 978-0-89239-308-4
51095
9 780892 393084